To my young nephew, Leo. I dream of
and hope to share many adventures in the waves together!

To my dad, Fernando, who is the true gifted writer in the family,
thanks for the endless inspiration.

And to my sister, Tami, a passionate preschool teacher who
helped me learn the world of picture books like no one else could.
—M. G.

To Fabian
—R. K.

The illustrations for this book were made digitally with various analog textures.

Cataloging-in-Publication Data has been applied for and may be obtained from the Library of Congress.

ISBN 978-1-4197-6000-6

Text and illustrations © 2022 Maya Gabeira
Book design by Heather Kelly

Printed and bound in China
10 9 8 7 6 5 4 3 2 1

Abrams Books for Young Readers are available at special discounts when purchased in quantity for premiums
and promotions as well as fundraising or educational use. Special editions can also be created to specification.
For details, contact specialsales@abramsbooks.com or the address below.

Abrams® is a registered trademark of Harry N. Abrams, Inc.

ABRAMS The Art of Books
195 Broadway, New York, NY 10007
abramsbooks.com

MAYA
and the Beast

Written by
Maya Gabeira

Illustrated by
Ramona Kaulitzki

Abrams Books for Young Readers • New York

ONCE UPON A TIME, in a fishing village called Nazaré, there lived a Beast.

This Beast wasn't an animal or a monster. It was a wave made of water.

And not just any wave: On special winter days, it could be taller than a seven-story building. Taller than the Christ in Rio de Janeiro or the Tower of London. Bigger than a blue whale, the biggest animal to ever exist!

When it crashed, it made a loud and scary sound. The people of Nazaré could hear it from their homes. Tucked into their beds at night, they could feel the windows shake and the ground vibrate from the Beast.

In that same village lived a young girl named Maya. Maya was shy and felt most secure hiding behind her mom's skirt, telling stories to her dad, or playing with her dogs, Naza and Stormy.

Maya also had asthma. She often felt difficulty breathing, and she took her medicine with her everywhere she went. When her chest got tight and her asthma kicked in, she couldn't play outside with her friends, and she felt fragile and scared. She wished she could breathe better.

But there was one thing that made Maya feel strong, and that was sports. She loved dancing and gymnastics and especially swimming—nothing compared to the feeling of being in the water.

Maya had heard about the Beast in her village. She had heard the scary sounds it made. Since she was little, she'd heard the stories warning her against ever getting close to the big waves of Nazaré.

But that didn't stop Maya from looking for adventure—she wanted to see the Beast up close for herself. So one day, Maya ventured out with Naza and Stormy. She headed in a direction she had never gone before, and soon she found herself on a tall cliff.

Maya stood on the cliff and looked out toward the water. She felt the cold wind and watched the huge waves. The Beast wasn't ugly or scary like she had been told—quite the opposite. It was the most beautiful thing Maya had ever seen.

The power of the waves, the sound of them crashing against the rocks, the shades of blue, the spray of water. She was mesmerized.

And there was something else, too: There were boys in that water! They were gliding across the waves, tiny creatures against the blue. The speed at which those brave boys were riding down the Beast—it was the first time she had ever seen surfing.

Maya had never felt anything so exciting. It was love at first sight.

When she got home, she told her dad what she had witnessed.
"Daddy, I've discovered my dream— it's surfing! It's a sport where the boys ride the waves. It's the coolest thing I've ever seen."

Maya's dad didn't know much about surfing, but he could sense his daughter's passion. And the next morning . . .

Maya found a gift.

She was so happy, she ran with her surfboard all the way to the town beach, where small waves broke on the shore. There were the boys again, surfing and laughing and having the best time. Maya gathered her courage and approached one of them. She asked him to teach her to surf. But the boy looked at her and said, "This is no place for you. Surfing is too dangerous for girls."

Maya was heartbroken. How could she ever surf the Beast if no one would teach her—even on the small waves?

The next day, Maya climbed the cliff again. There she found a beautiful shell. She picked it up and put it to her ear, and beneath the rush of waves, she heard . . .

Maya, if you dream of surfing, you must keep trying.
You will fall many times, but don't give up.
Many will tell you this sport isn't for girls, but don't believe them.
Anyone who works hard can become a great surfer.
YOU can become a great surfer, Maya.

Maya looked out over the water, and she knew the Beast was calling to her. She felt the calming presence of the waves—and a new strength inside herself. Facing the Beast, she didn't feel shy or scared. And she knew she couldn't just sit and watch anymore.

With new determination, Maya tucked her surfboard under her arm and ran back to

. . . and she ran there every day after that.

She swam and swam and swam, even when she felt out of breath and cold. At first, it was scary holding her breath underwater. But because of her asthma, every time she had to dive under a wave, she knew how the breathlessness would feel. And the more she swam, the less she felt the squeeze on her chest. What she'd thought was her weakness was becoming a strength.

She practiced popups on her board in the sand. Each time she fell, she got up again.

Ignoring the looks of the older boys, she dragged her board out into the small waves, and she kept practicing.

As Maya grew stronger and more confident on her surfboard, her determination and passion grew, too. She felt resilient. She felt powerful. She felt happy.

One day, she returned to the cliff, looking for that special shell. When she found it and put it to her ear, she heard:

The Beast is proud of you, Maya.
Never give up on your dreams, and be kind to those who will help
you along the way.

All of us are tiny creatures in a big world.
But even the tiniest of people can have bravery as big as the sea.

Maya closed her eyes and listened to the crashing water. She knew she needed the sea and the waves as much as she needed breath in her lungs.

She was going to be a great surfer, a champion, and no one could stop her. She might surprise everyone with what she would accomplish—but not the Beast. She dreamed of the day she would prove that a girl could ride the biggest wave in the world.

And one day . . .

She did.

Author's Note

I grew up in Rio de Janeiro, Brazil, and I fell in love with surfing at my local beach, Ipanema, at fourteen years old. My friends surfed—but they were all boys. I'd always been given the strong impression that surfing was not a girl's sport. But something about the ocean, the freedom, and navigating a male-dominated world captured my imagination. I jumped in headfirst, ignoring the limitations that I and my family believed I had as an asthmatic child.

I started by learning from a surf school in my area, and from there, I adventured out into the big world. At fifteen, I was studying and surfing abroad in Australia. At seventeen, I moved to Hawaii, the most famous place for surfing in the world. I was inspired when I saw Jamilah Star, one of the only women surfing big waves at the time, carrying her huge gun surfboard—a board shaped specifically to catch big waves—across the sand in Waimea Bay: one brave woman in the middle of many brave men. From there, I continued to travel and to surf the most beautiful and famous waves.

Today I live in Nazaré, Portugal, like the Maya in this story. I became a professional big wave surfer, the first woman pro in my sport, back in 2007. Eleven years later, at Praia do Norte in Nazaré, I surfed a 68-foot wave, the biggest of my life so far—and the biggest ever surfed by a woman. I petitioned the World Surf League to establish the first women's record—after many years of only men being honored—and set the first Guinness World Record for the largest wave surfed by a female surfer. I then broke my own record in 2020, also in Nazaré, by surfing the biggest wave of the year—male *or* female—measured at 73.5 feet.

Many didn't believe it to be possible, including myself at the lowest moments of my career: a woman beating men in big wave surfing, a sport that is still heavily male-dominated. A sport that can be dangerous, but that celebrates courage, force, and power—all attributes not easily associated with or celebrated in women in our society.

But this wasn't the first time I'd surfed at Nazaré. Years earlier, when I displayed bravery in the waves and failed, nearly drowning while surfing a huge wave there, I was heavily criticized and told I had been unprepared. I endured four years of spinal surgeries, physical and emotional traumas, doubts, and uncertainties. Meanwhile, I watched as my male peers were praised for their bravery, never having their abilities brought into question. In those years, I could have given up—decided that I couldn't continue anymore, physically or emotionally. Instead, I took my time, studied my weaknesses, and strengthened my game. I dove deep into the quest of bettering myself and continued to pursue my dream of dominating the Beast: the waves of Nazaré.

As a young woman in the world, I learned to be independent, to speak up for myself, and to fight for what really matters. And I know I am where I am today because I was inspired to dream by my dad. He is a liberal journalist and politician, and I moved in with him when I was thirteen years old. He taught me, through action, that dedication, passion, and hard work are the recipe for a fulfilling life. My family also allowed me to adventure into the world alone, to explore without setting any limitations or imposing their expectations on me. And so I grew up eager to find my true self, to follow my own path, and to see the world.

Though *Maya and the Beast* is fictionalized—the fairytale version of my childhood and my discovery of surfing—it is still my story. Through it, I want to share with all kids—including my loving nephew, Leo, who is five now—that our dreams can come true if we persist. I was challenged and doubted, I fell, I cried, but I never allowed it to stop me. I turned it all into opportunities, life lessons, and fire. I am grateful, because although my path hasn't been easy, it has been rich, unique, and intense. We must encourage kids to go after their dreams, to discover their true selves. To experiment, to fail, to get back up, and to never ever give up. And especially to the girls: Your bravery, curiosity, and willingness to challenge yourselves should always be encouraged and never doubted.